BOOK 3b

The Ladybird Key Words Reading Scheme

Boys and girls

by W. MURRAY

with illustrations by MARTIN AITCHISON

Ladybird Books

Peter and Jane are
at home.

They are at play.

Look at this, says Peter.

We like to jump.

We can jump on this.

We can have some fun
on this.

at play on

Peter and Jane like
to play.

I want to jump on this,
says Peter.

Look at me, Jane.

Look at me.

Up I go.

Up and up I go.

It's fun to play on this.

---

me Up up

Jane wants to play.

I want to play, please,
Jane says.

Peter, I want to jump,
please.

Jane jumps up and down.

Up and down I go,
Jane says.

Up and down, up and
down.

Look at me, Peter.

---

please down

Peter likes to help.

He sees Daddy go up.

He wants to help Daddy.

I want to help you,
he says.

Please can I help you?

Yes, says Daddy, you can
help me.

---

help sees Daddy

Here comes Jane with some tea.

This is for you, Daddy, Jane says.

Here you are. Here's some tea for you. Come down for the tea, please.

Daddy sees Jane with the tea, and comes down.

with tea

Here's Daddy with some apples.

Peter has an apple, and Jane has an apple.

Peter and Jane see Daddy go up and down.

They want to help Daddy with the apples.

---

an apple apples

Peter and Jane are in the car with Daddy.

They like it in the car.

Mummy is at home.

They see a toy shop and a sweet shop.

Peter wants to see the school.

---

car Mummy school

They go on to the school.

Here it is, says Peter,
here's the school.

Peter and Jane like the
school.

Here's a cake shop,
says Daddy.

Mummy wants some cakes.

We have to get cakes
for tea.

---

cake cakes get

CLAREC
UHD 905 K

Here we are at home, says Daddy.

Peter helps Daddy with the car, and Jane helps Mummy get the tea.

Good girl, says Mummy to Jane.

You are a good girl to help me like this.

Good good girl

Jane and Peter like to
play with the rabbits.

Peter has one, and Jane
has one.

They are good to the
rabbits.

Peter's rabbit can jump,
and Jane's rabbit
can jump.

The rabbits like Peter
and Jane.

---

rabbit rabbits one

Here's a home for the rabbits.

Daddy helps Peter with it, and the dog looks on.

It's Pat. He's a good dog.

Pat likes rabbits.

He likes to play with the rabbits.

BIR

Peter and Jane have some flowers.

Jane says, Girls like flowers.

Peter says, Yes, and boys like flowers.

Jane wants to have a flower shop.

Peter helps with it.

He gets some red flowers for Jane.

---

flowers boys red

Here's a tree, says Jane, and here are some flowers.

Come and look, Peter.

Look at the red flowers and the tree.

Peter looks.

Yes, he says, I like the tree and I like the flowers.

This is a boat, says Peter,
a boat on the water.

Here's a man in a boat.

A boy is with the man.

Have a look, Jane.

Have a look at this red
boat on the water.

---

boat man

I want a boat, says Peter.

I want one to play with.

Please help me, Daddy.

Please help me with this.

I want some help with this.

Yes, says Daddy, I want to
help you with the boat.

Here's Peter with the boat.

It's a red one.

He wants to go to the water with the boat.

Daddy gets the car to go to the water.

Jane is in the car.

Here they are, at the water.

Peter is in the water with the red boat.

He has fun in the water with the boat.

Can you see a fish in the water? says Jane.

No, says Peter.

Peter sees a man and
a boy.

The man has a boat.

It's a Police boat.

Peter says to Jane,
Look at that boat.

That man has a Police
boat.

I like that Police boat.

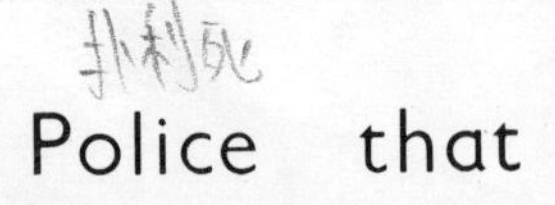

Police that

This is the school.

The boys and girls are at school.

Here are the Police.

The Police are at the school.

They have come in a Police car.

They have come to help the boys and girls.

POLICE

Peter has a toy car.

Jane is with Peter.

Jane says, Here's a shop with apples.

Please get some apples, Peter.

Go into this shop for some apples.

Yes, we want some apples, says Peter.

Peter and Jane want to go to the station to see the trains.

They like to look at the trains at the station.

Here they go, on a bus to the station.

It's a red bus.

They like it on the bus.

---

station train trains bus

REQUEST
STOP

The bus has come to the station.

Peter and Jane go into the station.

They like to see the trains.

I like to go on a train with Mummy and Daddy, says Jane.

Yes, it's fun to go on a train, says Peter.

2
V 12

The boy and the girl
are at home.

It was fun at the station,
says Jane.

Yes, it was fun to see the
trains, says Peter.

He gives a ball to Pat.

Mummy gives Peter an
apple, and gives some
cakes to Jane.

---

was gives

The toys go in here, says Jane.

Mummy says, You have to go to bed, Jane.

You have to go to bed, Peter.

Come on, up to bed you go.

You are a good girl, Jane, and you are a good boy, Peter.

---

bed

New words used in this book

Page		*Page*	
4	at play on	28	—
6	me up	30	boat man
8	please down	32	—
10	help sees Daddy	34	—
12	with tea	36	—
14	an apple	38	Police that
16	car Mummy school	40	—
18	cake get	42	—
20	good girl	44	station train bus
22	rabbits one	46	—
24	—	48	was gives
26	flowers boys red	50	bed

Total number of new words 36

The vocabulary of this book is the same as that of the parallel reader 3a.